NO LONGER PROPERTY OF
ANYTHINK LIBRARIES/
RANGEVIEW LIBRARY DISTRICT

Bartholomew Bug
A Zombie with Different Cravings

Written by the Lively:
Crystal Marcos

Illustrated by the (Re)Animated:
Marie Marcos

D0118280

Dedication
For Kaylee, Maxwell, and Alyssa
Not All Zombies Have to Bite!

Note from the author: This book was created because my daughter woke up one morning and told me about a nightmare of being chased by zombies. I was surprised because I didn't realize she even knew about zombies—let alone being afraid of them. I started mulling this over and decided she didn't have to be afraid. So I introduced Bartholomew to her and her cousins, all of whom were four years old at the time. They loved Bartholomew even before I had a picture to show them. No more nightmares! I also enjoyed working with my sister on this project! It's a family affair.

Copyright © 2017 by Crystal Marcos

All rights reserved. No part of this book may be reproduced in any form or by any electronic or mechanical means, including information storage and retrieval systems, without permission in writing from the publisher, except by a reviewer, who may quote passages in a review.

Cat Marcs Publishing
PO Box 54
Silverdale, WA 98383

www.CatMarcs.com

Printed in the United States of America

Library of Congress Control Number: 2017905301
Cat Marcs Publishing, Silverdale, WA

ISBN 978-1-943786-02-2

Bartholomew Buggins is who I am.
When you see me, you don't need to scram.

I'm not after what lies in your head.
So please—don't be filled with such dread.

You won't have to keep me away.
Let's try to become pals today.

Although I'm a zombie, it's true,
I'll never be munching on you.

This may come as a colossal surprise,
but I'd rather eat cookies and pies.

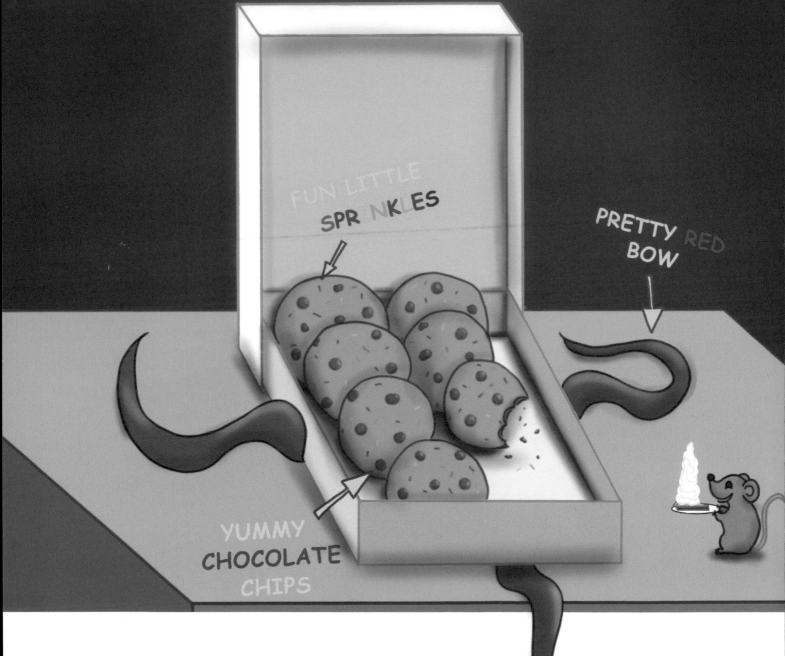

For cookies have fun little sprinkles
instead of those boring brain wrinkles.

And my favorite part of a pie
is whipped cream piled high to the sky!

I'll tell you what makes me unique.
Come see, I will give you a peek.

I think brains are an excellent tool.
I practice math skills on my stool.

I am a distinguished young fellow.
Unlike other zombies, I'm mellow.

Those monsters are really quite loud
so it's hard to fit in with that crowd.

I'd much rather be reading a book
somewhere in a nice peaceful nook.

Or strolling along down the street,
waving hello to the people I meet.

Expressing myself is the key,
to show others much more about me.

I let my creative side shine,
I read poems aloud that are mine.

On Sundays, I love planting trees,
my fingers in dirt and scuffed knees.

There's a neighbor I'm trying to show,
his trees for some reason won't grow.

My body is covered in grime.
Yet I'll show you a wonderful time.

I'll wear my most marvelous suit.
My purple bow tie is a hoot.

If you come to the diner at night,
I hope I won't give you a fright.

I'll split up my jello with you.
They serve me with plenty for two.

Perhaps we could dine at Chef Sally
on the corner—it's right up the alley.

Let's have a warm cup of mint tea.
For tea is so soothing to me.

You should know I'm a mess when I drink.
If I were a boat I would sink.

The holes in my chest make tea spout.
The liquid goes in and leaks out.

I have truly enjoyed meeting you.
But now, I must bid you adieu!

It's late and my cat needs to eat.
You'd like her—she's really quite sweet.

I believe that our friendship will bloom.
For a friend just like you I have room.

Can you spot the hidden brains?
What else do you see?

For more of Bartholomew Buggins
and fun activities, please visit
http://crystalmarcos.com/bb/buggins.html

Award-winning author Crystal Marcos has been a storyteller her entire life. As the oldest of five children, she had to do a lot of entertaining. Crystal is the author of two children's books, *BELLYACHE: A Delicious Tale* and *HEADACHE: The Hair-Raising Sequel to BELLYACHE*. She recently wrote her first Young Adult novel, *Novus (The Cresecren Chronicles, Book 1)*. *Bartholomew Buggins: A Zombie with Different Cravings* is her first picture book. She lives in Washington State with her husband, daughter Kaylee, and son Jaxon.

Please visit her: http://www.crystalmarcos.com/

Marie Marcos is Crystal Marcos' youngest sister. Marie's creations have graced the covers of two of her sister's books. She is thrilled to illustrate Bartholomew Buggins and work side-by-side with Crystal to make him come to life. Marie served in the US Navy before continuing her education at Western Washington University. She resides in Washington State.

CPSIA information can be obtained at www.ICGtesting.com
Printed in the USA
LVIW01n1447190917
549277LV00009B/88